A Note to Parents and Caregivers:

Read-it! Readers are for children who are just starting on the amazing road to reading. These beautiful books support both the acquisition of reading skills and the love of books.

 The PURPLE LEVEL presents basic topics and objects using high frequency words and simple language patterns.

 The RED LEVEL presents familiar topics using common words and repeating sentence patterns.

 The BLUE LEVEL presents new ideas using a larger vocabulary and varied sentence structure.

 The YELLOW LEVEL presents more challenging ideas, a broad vocabulary, and wide variety in sentence structure.

 The GREEN LEVEL presents more complex ideas, an extended vocabulary range, and expanded language structures.

 The ORANGE LEVEL presents a wide range of ideas and concepts using challenging vocabulary and complex language structures.

When sharing a book with your child, read in short stretches, pausing often to talk about the pictures. Have your child turn the pages and point to the pictures and familiar words. And be sure to reread favorite stories or parts of stories.

There is no right or wrong way to share books with children. Find time to read with your child, and pass on the legacy of literacy.

Adria F. Klein, Ph.D.
Professor Emeritus
California State University
San Bernardino, California

Editor: Jill Kalz
Designer: Amy Muehlenhardt
Page Production: Lori Bye
Art Director: Nathan Gassman
Associate Managing Editor: Christianne Jones
The illustrations in this book were created with watercolor and pencil.

Picture Window Books
151 Good Counsel Drive
P.O. Box 669
Mankato, MN 56002-0669
877-845-8392
www.capstonepub.com

Printed in the United States of America in Stevens Point, Wisconsin.
072010
005880R

Library of Congress Cataloging-in-Publication Data
Klein, Adria F. (Adria Fay), 1947–
Max stays overnight / by Adria F. Klein ; illustrated by Mernie Gallagher-Cole.
p. cm. — (Read-it! readers. The life of Max)
Summary: Most of the time, Max's friend DeShawn lives far away with his father,
but this weekend he is staying with his mother and has invited Max to join him for
a sleepover.
ISBN-13: 978-1-4048-3149-0 (library binding)
ISBN-10: 1-4048-3149-5 (library binding)
ISBN-13: 978-1-4048-3547-4 (paperback)
ISBN-10: 1-4048-3547-4 (paperback)
[1. Friendship—Fiction. 2. Sleepovers—Fiction. 3. Divorce—Fiction. 4. Hispanic
Americans—Fiction. 5. African Americans—Fiction.] I. Gallagher-Cole, Mernie, ill.
II. Title.
PZ7.K678324Mayf 2006
[E]—dc22   2006027299

Max
Stays Overnight

by Adria F. Klein
illustrated by Mernie Gallagher-Cole

Special thanks to our advisers for their expertise:

Adria F. Klein, Ph.D.
Professor Emeritus, California State University
San Bernardino, California

Susan Kesselring, M.A.
Literacy Educator
Rosemount–Apple Valley–Eagan (Minnesota) School District

PICTURE WINDOW BOOKS
a capstone imprint

Max and DeShawn are good friends.

4

Max and DeShawn used to live next to each other. They were in the same class in school.

Then DeShawn moved away to
live with his dad.

6

DeShawn lives with his dad
most of the time.

But he stays with his mom every
other weekend.

Max calls DeShawn. He asks DeShawn to come over on Friday.

DeShawn says he can't. He will be
at his dad's house on Friday.

DeShawn says he will be at his mom's apartment next Friday.

DeShawn asks Max if Max can come and stay overnight then.

Max asks his mom. She says yes.
Max is very happy!

14

15

The next Friday, Max goes next door.
DeShawn is there.

Max and DeShawn walk to the park.
They play cards.

Later, they watch a funny movie about a talking dog.

They eat popcorn and drink
grape juice.

They talk about school, sports, and their favorite TV shows.

They make a tent on DeShawn's bed.

Max is glad when DeShawn stays
with his mom. Max and DeShawn
are good friends.

23